August

IT'S BRAMBLE TIME!
(don't over do it.
remember those
gurgly tummies last year)

THOUGHt I'd Treat
Myself & visit you
guys. How about
Like this Thursday
Love & hugs,

Reg x

Monday	Tuesday	Wednesday	Thursday	Friday	Saturday	Sunday	NOTES
		1	2	3	4 Grasshopper Bingo at 6:00 pm Trevor presiding take Pencils	5	If anybody finds a jar of damson jelly it's mine. Polecat Mae
6	7	8	9 midnight Feast 11:30 bring candles	10	11	12	
13	14 MOLE RACES!	15	16	17	18	19	THEY ALL SAY THAT.
20	21	22 Reg coming to enjoy 'the Forest Vibe'	23	24	25	26 fete at the old barn donations for raffle Welcome	It's true. Hands off PM
27	29	28	30	31 done →	send lavender soap (and other unwanted Xmas presents)		

The Hubble & Hattie imprint was launched in 2009, and is named in memory of two very special Westie sisters owned by Veloce's proprietors. Since the first book, many more have been added, all with the same objective: to be of real benefit to the species they cover; at the same time promoting compassion, understanding and respect between all animals (including human ones!)

Our new range of books for kids will champion the same values and standards that we've always held dear, but to the adults of the future. Children will love reading these beautifully illustrated, carefully crafted publications, or read to them, absorbing valuable life lessons whilst being highly entertained. We've more great books already in the pipeline so remember to check out our website for details.

Other books from our Hubble & Hattie Kids! imprint

9781787111608 9781787112926 9781787113060 9781787113077 9781787114302

9781787113121 9781787115156 9781787113862 9781787114180

www.hubbleandhattie.com

First published October 2019 by Veloce Publishing Limited, Veloce House, Parkway Farm Business Park, Middle Farm Way, Poundbury, Dorchester, Dorset, DT1 3AR, England. Tel 01305 260068/Fax 01305 250479/email info@hubbleandhattie.com/web www.hubbleandhattie. com ISBN: 978-1-787115-16-3 UPC: 6-36847-01516-9 © Chantal Bourgonje, David Hoskins & Veloce Publishing Ltd 2019. All rights reserved. With the exception of quoting brief passages for the purpose of review, no part of this publication may be recorded, reproduced or transmitted by any means, including photocopying, without the written permission of Veloce Publishing Ltd. Throughout this book logos, model names and designations, etc, have been used for the purposes of identification, illustration and decoration. Such names are the property of the trademark holder as this is not an official publication. Readers with ideas for books about animals, or animal-related topics, are invited to write to the publisher of Veloce Publishing at the above address. British Library Cataloguing in Publication Data – A catalogue record for this book is available from the British Library. Typesetting, design and page make-up all by Veloce Publishing Ltd on Apple Mac. Printed in India by Parksons Graphics

Positive thinking for Piglets

Horace & Nim

Chantal Bourgonje and David Hoskins

KiDS
Hubble & Hattie

Kay was in a bad mood.

She'd been trying to pluck an acorn from an oak tree all morning, but it was just out of reach.

"You don't want it badly enough," said a voice.

It was Kay's cool cousin, Reg.

"Are you collecting for an acorn pie? They're my favourite."

Kay had never heard of acorn pie. It sounded delicious.

"You know you can get anything you want if you want it badly enough, right?" said Reg.

"Try it. Close those peepers and concentrate on really, really wanting that acorn."

So Kay closed her peepers. And concentrated on really, really wanting that acorn.

"Now open them," said Reg.

And there it was.

"But you just picked it off the tree and gave it to me," said Kay.

"The magic of positive thinking works in mysterious ways," said Reg. "Catch you later."

And off he went.

It was a pretty amazing idea.

Could you really get anything you wanted?

If you wanted it badly enough?

Kay closed her eyes
and concentrated on
really, really wanting
an acorn pie.

And when she
opened them ...

There was Polecat Mac.

"Wow," said Kay. "I was just wishing for an acorn pie and there you are, the best baker in the forest. It must mean you're going to bake me an acorn pie."

"I'm far too busy today," said Polecat Mac. "Baking you an acorn pie is the last thing I'd do."

And off he went.

"Perhaps ...

Maybe ...

I didn't try
hard enough
at wanting it,"
thought Kay

So she tried wanting it again, even harder.

And this time when she opened her eyes ...

Nim and Edie were standing there.

"You don't have an acorn pie for me by any chance?" asked Kay.

They didn't.

Kay was disappointed. She told her friends how cousin Reg had talked about the magic of positive thinking, but how it wasn't really working for her.

"Maybe it means," said Edie, "that if you want something badly enough, you'll put enough effort into getting it. Like with an acorn pie, you'd bake one yourself."

"I was thinking more of eating it than baking it," said Kay.

"There's always Horace's kitchen," said Nim. "We could learn to bake together," said Edie. "It'd be fun."

"Hmmm," said Kay, not convinced.

Horace was pleased to see them, and said he had a
recipe for acorn pie.

They found all
the ingredients.

They all helped put
the recipe together.

And forty minutes
later ...

... out of Horace's oven came a beautiful acorn pie.

It smelled fantastic!

And then there was a knock on the door.

It was Polecat Mac. "Is Kay here?" he asked.

Before anyone could reply, there was a familiar voice from behind him.

"Do I smell baking?" It was Kay's cousin Reg again.

Kay jumped outside to show him.

"Look," said Kay. "We baked an acorn pie."

"Oh wow!" said Reg. "You remembered my birthday."

It was an awkward moment.

"And you remembered that acorn pie is my favourite! That is SO KIND," said Reg.

And he took the pie.

"That's the magic of positive thinking," said Reg. "I've been wishing for an acorn pie all day. And there it is!"

He thanked Kay again. And then off he went with the pie: Kay's delicious, freshly-baked, fantastically-smelling acorn pie.

And no one knew what to say.

"Well, at least Reg
is happy," said Kay
eventually, trying to
smile. "And at least I've
learned how to bake so
I suppose I could
always ...
bake another?"

"You know I said baking an acorn pie would be the last thing I'd do today," said Polecat Mac. "Well, I'd done everything else I had to do, so I did it." "For me?" said Kay.

"That's the nicest thing EVER!" And she gave the polecat a big hug. "Don't overdo it," said Polecat Mac.

He sometimes felt a bit awkward when other creatures said nice things to him. "It's no big deal," he said.

But it was. Kay had
discovered a new favourite
dish. She wasn't sure
about the magic of positive
thinking ...

But she was absolutely certain about acorn pies.

She was their number one fan.